The SUPERDUPER COLLECTOR

Written by Susan Cornell Poskanzer
Illustrated by Paul Harvey

Troll Associates

Library of Congress Cataloging in Publication Data

Poskanzer, Susan Cornell.
   The superduper collector.

   Summary: When she runs out of space for all the
things that she collects, Whitney Squirrel decides to
make more room by moving her sleeping brother outside
and using up the available space in her parents' room.
   [1. Squirrels—Fiction. 2. Collectors and collecting—Fiction] I. Harvey, Paul, 1926-   ill.
II. Title.
PZ7.P8382St   1986   [E]   85-14051
ISBN 0-8167-0606-9 (lib. bdg.)
ISBN 0-8167-0607-7 (pbk.)

The SUPERDUPER COLLECTOR

Whitney Squirrel was a
superduper collector. She had
the very finest collection of nuts.

She saved every button and
paper clip she found. She kept
the string from every package
she got. Visitors came from miles
around to see her collections.

Whitney's family was proud of
her. They liked having a famous
squirrel in the family. They liked
helping Whitney with her
collections. But there was one
problem. She had so many things
that her room was a mess.

"Whitney, your room looks
terrible," said her father, Leon.
"You MUST clean it up."
"Your string is getting all mixed
up with your buttons. Your
buttons are getting all mixed up
with your string," said her
mother, Shirley.
"I can't even see my half of the
room," cried Barney, her little
brother.

Whitney looked around the
room. It was true. Her
wonderful collections were
getting all mixed up. There were
nuts in her paper clips. There
were paper clips in her nuts.

"Yes, you are right," she said.
"I will clean up my things."

That very night she put
everything in its own place.
Buttons went into a button box.
Nuts went into a nut basket.
Paper clips went into a paper-
clip can. Whitney rolled all the
string into one big ball.
Everything was neat.

"Your room looks wonderful,"
said Whitney's father.
"There is not one bit of string in
your buttons," said her mother.
"I can find my bed again," said
Barney.

Whitney smiled. It felt good to
be a famous squirrel who had a
neat room.

16

Whitney looked at her room. She
noticed something important.
"There is more space when
things are neat," said Whitney.
"Now I can collect more things."

Whitney was a superduper collector. She collected golden rocks from the riverbed. She collected fine spider webs from windowsills. She collected colorful stamps from letters her Aunt Doris sent her. She even started collecting red socks. She found all these things. And she added them to her collection. "This is the best collection in the world—the neatest, too," said Whitney.
She felt wonderful. But there was one problem.

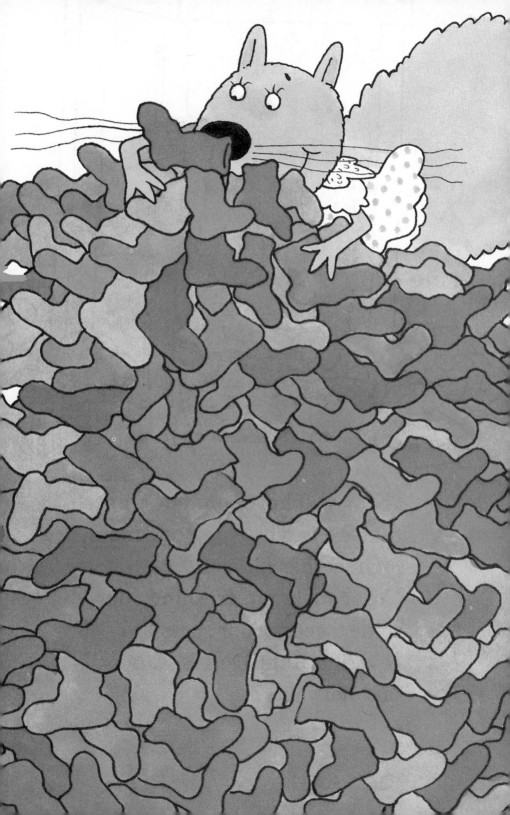

"Now you have so many things
that we can't get in your room,"
moaned her father.
"Your rocks are crushing your
spider webs. Your socks are
covering Aunt Doris's stamps,"
said her mother.

"There is no room for me at all!"
complained Barney.
"Yes, you are right," said
Whitney. "My room is too full.
I must do something."

21

That night Whitney couldn't fall
asleep. She lay in her bed.
"What will I do?" she asked.
"Where will I put all my
things?"

She looked around the room. She
saw Barney. He was snoring. It
was true. There was NOT
enough room for Barney. She
had an idea.

Whitney took a big sheet
outside. She hammered it up
between two strong trees. Then
she tried out the hammock she
had made. It rocked gently.

"This will be perfect for
Barney," she said.
She carried her sleeping brother
out to the hammock.
"He looks just fine out here,"
said Whitney. "He will like his
new bed when he wakes up."

Back in her room Whitney
spread out her collections.
"This is fine," said Whitney.
"But it could be better. If I had
more space, I could see more of
my things."

She looked at her mother and father. They were sleeping. There was plenty of space in their room. So she put her spider webs on her mother's table. Her stamps and red socks fit perfectly on her father's bookcase.

Whitney looked around her own
room. There was plenty of
space.
Whitney looked outside. A full
moon lit up the sky. It lit up the
whole neighborhood.

"A perfect night for collecting,"
thought Whitney.
Whitney went outside.
"It's easy to find things in the
bright moonlight," said
Whitney. "Especially for a
superduper collector like me."

She found bright leaves that glowed in the moonlight. She collected sixteen lightning bugs in one glass jar. She found enough pine cones to fill five shopping bags. She even found some shiny shells and two red socks.

"I can use these," she said.
Whitney worked all night. She
put away everything neatly in
her room.
"This is really the best collection
in the world," she thought.
Then she fell asleep.

Leon woke up early. He opened
his eyes. He could not believe
what he saw. Stamps, spider
webs, and red socks were
everywhere.
"I think we have a problem
here," he said to Shirley.
Shirley opened her eyes. She saw
the spider webs and she sneezed.

They went into Whitney's room.
Whitney was sleeping. Her new
things were everywhere.

"I wonder where Barney is,"
said Shirley.
Barney came in, rubbing his
eyes. He did not look happy.

Whitney woke up with a smile.
She looked at her father. He was
not smiling. Whitney looked at
her mother. She was not smiling.
Whitney looked at Barney.
Barney was not smiling.

"Did you see my new things?"
asked Whitney. She was very
excited.

"I saw them," said her father.

"I saw them," said her mother.

"I saw them," said Barney.

"There is one problem," said
Whitney's father.
"There is MORE than one
problem," cried Barney.

40

"You have too many things!"
shouted Whitney's mother.
"I want to sleep in the house,"
said Barney. "I don't want to
sleep outside in a hammock."

Whitney looked at her family.
She knew they were right.
"But what will I do with all my
wonderful things?" Whitney
asked. "I don't want to throw
them out."

They all thought. Then her
father smiled.
"You could share your things
with other squirrels," he said.
"Yes," said Whitney's mother.
"Why not give some things to
your friends? And to other
squirrels who don't have as
much as you do."
"Squirrels who still have room to
sleep in their homes," added
Barney.

And that is what Whitney did. She gave away the buttons, paper clips, shells, string, stamps, and leaves. She gave away the pine cones, rocks, lightning bugs, and spider webs. She kept the nuts and the red socks for herself.

The other squirrels promised to take good care of Whitney's things. They told Whitney she could see the things whenever she wanted.

And why did Whitney agree to
this plan? It was simple.
Whitney was a superduper
collector.

"Finding things is the best part,"
she said. "Now I can start all
over again."
And that is just what she did.